First published in the United States, Great Britain, Canada, Australia, and New Zealand in 2011 by
North-South Books, Inc., an imprint of NordSüd Verlag AG, CH-8005 Zürich, Switzerland.

Translated by David Henry Wilson. Edited by Susan Pearson.
Designed by Pamela Darcy.
Distributed in the United States by North-South Books Inc., New York 10017.
Library of Congress Cataloging-in-Publication Data is available.
Printed in Germany by Grafisches Centrum Cuno GmbH & Co. KG, 39240 Calbe, June 2011.
ISBN: 978-0-7358-4045-4 (trade edition)
1 3 5 7 9 • 10 8 6 4 2
www.northsouth.com

FSC
www.fsc.org
MIX
Paper from
responsible sources
FSC® C043106

by Wolfram Hänel ❄ *illustrated by* Judith Rossell

Merry Christmas, Mr. Snowman!

NorthSouth
New York / London

It was Christmas Day, and the snow was falling in thick, wet flakes. Pip and Squeak were waiting for the time when they would light the tree and open their presents. Squeak hopped from one foot to the other. Pip could hardly keep still either.

Suddenly Pip had an idea. "Come on, Squeak!" he cried. "Let's build a snowman!"

In no time at all Pip and Squeak rolled a huge snowball. Then they made another for the snowman's belly and a third for the snowman's head.

Squeak tied her scarf around the snowman's neck, and
Pip fetched Grandpa's old hat from the garden shed.

"Finished!" shouted Pip as he carefully stuck a carrot
on the snowman's face for a nose.

"Time to come in!" Mommy Mouse called from the house.
"We're almost ready to begin."

"We're coming!" Pip shouted, but Squeak grabbed his arm.

"Wait!" she cried. "We can't leave Mr. Snowman out here all alone. He'll be sad if he doesn't have anyone to celebrate Christmas with."

"He might catch cold, too," said Pip. "I know what we can do!"

Pip ran to the garage to get the sled. Together, Pip and Squeak tipped Mr. Snowman onto it, but as they tipped—**PLOP!**—Mr. Snowman's head fell off.

"Oh, dear!" said Squeak. "Hang on, Mr. Snowman! We'll put you back together when we get inside."

The sled was heavy, but they managed to drag it across the lawn and into the house.

"Quick!" whispered Pip. "Before they see us."

Pip and Squeak pushed and pulled Mr. Snowman
into the living room and put him back together again
behind the Christmas tree.

"Perfect!" said Squeak.
"We can hardly see *him*, but
he can see everything."
"And he won't catch cold,"
said Pip. Then he whispered,
"Merry Christmas, Mr. Snowman!"

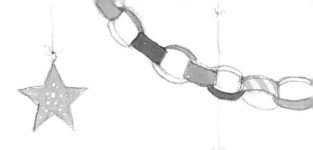

Pip and Squeak took the sled out to the yard. They were hardly back inside again when Mommy called, "Who wants to watch Daddy light the Christmas candles?"

"We do!" cried Pip and Squeak at the same time.

Daddy brought the matches. "We have to be really careful," he said. Then he looked down at his slippers in surprise. "What's this?" he asked. The toes of his slippers were soaking wet. There was a large puddle under the Christmas tree.

"There's someone behind the Christmas tree!"
said Mommy Mouse. "And he's wearing Grandpa's hat!"
Of course, Mommy and Daddy Mouse quickly
realized it wasn't Grandpa standing there. In the
warm room, the snowman had started to melt.
"How on earth did a snowman get into our living
room?" asked Daddy Mouse.

"Maybe Santa Claus brought him?" said Pip.

"I think it's more likely that he came in from the yard," said Mommy. "Perhaps on a sled?"

"And that's exactly where we're going to take him now," said Daddy. "A hot living room is no place for a snowman."

Mommy dried the floor while Daddy helped Pip and Squeak take the snowman back outside.

"Let's put him right in front of the window," said Squeak, "so he can see us inside."

Then they went back into the house to open their presents.

Pip got the new skis he was hoping for.
Squeak got a pair of skates, a drawing pad, and
a box of crayons in every color she could imagine.

Of course, Pip and Squeak had a present for Mommy and Daddy, too. It was a wooden nutcracker that looked like a cat. Everyone was happy. But still, something wasn't quite right. Pip and Squeak kept looking out the window at lonely Mr. Snowman.

"It must be terrible for him to see all this but not be able to join in," said Squeak.

"There's an icicle hanging from his nose," said Pip. "I think he's been crying."

Squeak felt like crying, too.

"But we can't bring him back into the living room," said Daddy Mouse. "A hot room is no place for a snowman."

Suddenly Pip laughed. "Then we have to do it the other way around!" he said.

"That's right!" cried Squeak. "If he can't come in, then we have to go out!"

So they all put on their coats, and hats, and boots and went outside. Mommy Mouse brought a lantern. Daddy Mouse brought a thermos of hot chocolate. Pip brought his new skis.

Then they all gathered around Mr. Snowman and started to sing Christmas carols.

"What on earth is going on over there?" called Mrs. Tillie from her window.

"We're celebrating Christmas with our snowman!" said Pip. "You can come, too! Mr. Snowman likes to have lots of people around."

More and more neighbors kept arriving to join in the singing. Mr. Snowman looked so happy Pip and Squeak thought he might start dancing.

"He's having a really good time," said Pip. "And the icicle has gone from his nose. He's stopped crying."

Squeak ran back into the living room for her sketch pad and crayons. Then she started to draw.

"I'm going to hang this picture in my room," she said. "Then in summer when it's so hot outside that everyone is complaining, I'll look at Mr. Snowman and think about today. Merry Christmas, Mr. Snowman!"